Billy & Rose

FOREVER FRIENDS

Billy & Rose

FOREVER FRIENDS

Amy Hest

illustrated by

Kady MacDonald Denton

CANDLEWICK PRESS

For Lev and Rosie and Frieda,
with love from Nonnie
AH

For B.B.
KMD

Text copyright © 2022 by Amy Hest
Illustrations copyright © 2022 by Kady MacDonald Denton

First edition 2022

Library of Congress Catalog Card Number 2021953317
ISBN 978-1-5362-1419-2

22 23 24 25 26 27 APS 10 9 8 7 6 5 4 3 2 1

Printed in Humen, Dongguan, China

This book was typeset in Utopia.
The illustrations were done in watercolor and ink.

Candlewick Press
99 Dover Street
Somerville, Massachusetts 02144

www.candlewick.com

CONTENTS

Chores and Cellos 1

How to Have a Catch 11

The Ice Cream Stand 21

The Sleepover 33

Chores and Cellos

One sunny morning, Rose hops out of bed bursting with energy and ready to play.

She looks for her favorite blue shorts to put on. And her favorite green shirt to put on. And her favorite red socks (they have ruffles). But all her favorites need washing.

I should do the wash, thinks Rose. And then she thinks, *Maybe later.*

She eats a carrot muffin instead of doing the wash . . .

reads a magazine instead of doing the wash . . .

and paints a picture instead of doing the wash.

She scrubs her face, and behind her ears.
Then Rose sighs a very big sigh that means
The time has come to do the wash.

So she gathers up her favorite blue shorts, her favorite green shirt, and the red socks with ruffles . . .

and carries them to the yard, where the
washtub and soapsuds are waiting.

"Hello, Rose!" Billy calls from the yard next door. "I've just finished my wash!" His clean clothes blow in the summer breeze.

"You do a good job," notes Rose.

"I know," agrees Billy. "I really enjoy my chores."

"What about that cello?" Rose points to the cello in the grass beside Billy. "I haven't heard you practice today."

"Maybe later," Billy tells Rose. "Practicing the cello is a very big chore."

"No, no," says Rose. "Doing the wash is a very big chore."

"If you want clean clothes," counsels Billy, "you have to do the wash."

"If you want to play glorious music," Rose counsels back, "you have to practice."

Billy looks at the cello. And Rose.

Rose looks at the washtub, the soapsuds, and Billy.

Then everyone gets to it. And for the rest of the morning, Rose does the wash to the glorious sound of Billy's cello.

How to Have a Catch

It is a fine fall day, and Billy and Rose are having a catch.

"Here comes the ball! Catch!" Rose calls.

Billy runs back . . . and back . . . and misses the ball.

"Don't worry, Billy. Next time," coaches Rose, "you will catch it."

Indeed, Billy thinks. *Next time.*

He throws the ball to Rose. "Catch, Rose! Catch!" he calls.

Rose runs back . . . and back . . . and misses the ball.

"There, there," coaches Billy. "You can do it, Rose."

Yes, thinks Rose, *I can.*

Billy and Rose throw and miss . . . throw and miss . . . throw and miss.

They have a little talk about how to have a catch.

"You throw too high," advises Rose. "That is the problem, my friend."

"You throw too low," advises Billy. "Try again, my friend."

Billy and Rose throw and miss . . . throw and miss . . . throw and miss.

They have a little talk about quitting.

"Guess what!" huffs Rose. "I quit!"

"Me too," Billy huffs back. "I quit now!"

And off they go, in opposite directions, until they each reach home.

Rose takes off her having-a-catch clothes. Then soaks in a nice warm bath. She soaks for a long time. Afterward, she pulls on some clean having-a-catch clothes and lounges on the couch with her library book. Every now and then, she sighs a soft sigh that means *Billy would like this book.*

Across the yard, Billy does a little swimming in a tubful of bubbles. Afterward, warm and dry, he sits at the window, knitting a new winter cap for Rose. *Oh, Rose*, Billy thinks.

Outside, the wind blows. Leaves blow. They fly and skip—red and yellow and purple—over two houses and the wavy grass.

Suddenly, Billy and Rose come sprinting across the yards.

"Let's have a catch," Rose calls to Billy.

"Now," Billy calls back. "Let's start now."

Billy and Rose throw and miss . . . throw and miss . . . and try, try, try.

"There, there," coaches Rose. "We can do it."

"One of these times," Billy coaches back, "we will catch the ball."

And finally, they do.

The Ice Cream Stand

It is a cold gray day, but Billy and Rose are putting the finishing touches on their ice cream stand. Red bowls! Blue spoons! Ice cream!

"It's the most beautiful ice cream stand I've ever seen," swoons Rose.

"A masterpiece," Billy swoons back. "Bring on the customers!"

Rose rings the little green bell. Then Billy rings the little green bell. And then they wait for customers.

They wait. And wait. And wait for customers.

"Patience," says Billy. A snowflake lands on the tip of his nose.

"Yes," agrees Rose. "Patience." A snowflake lands on the tip of her tongue.

But it is hard to be patient sometimes. So Billy and Rose sing a happy little jingle while they wait. "Ice cream! Ice cream! Come get your nice cold ice cream!" They sing and sing.

It is such a happy jingle, and they are very patient. Snowflakes fly by. But still no customers.

So Billy and Rose do jumping jacks while they wait. Ten in a row!

And hop around the yard. Twice without stopping!

And roll around the yard doing somersaults.

They are patient. More and more snowflakes
fly by. Billy's hat is white with snowflakes!
Rose's coat is white with snowflakes! But still
no customers.

"Perhaps it's too snowy for ice cream," says Billy.

"It is *never* too snowy for ice cream," says Rose.

Billy and Rose lean on their elbows. They watch the ice cream. And can't take their eyes off their snow-covered ice cream. They lean closer and closer, licking their lips and waiting for customers.

"I *need* a customer," mumbles Rose.

"And *I* need a customer," mumbles Billy.

They take turns ringing the little green bell. Snow floats from the sky. More and more snow. It is silent and beautiful. A masterpiece. Billy and Rose blink in the beautiful snow. They watch their beautiful ice cream, licking their lips.

"Maybe *I* can be your customer," whispers Rose.

"And maybe I can be *yours*," Billy whispers back.

"Now?" asks Rose.

"Now," says Billy.

So Billy serves Rose and Rose serves Billy, and everyone has a customer.

STORY 4

The Sleepover

It was a warm spring day, and soon it will be night. Time to go home. But Billy and Rose don't want to go home to their separate homes.

So they sit in the grass instead, and reminisce about their splendid day together. A day of running, skipping, and playing ball.

"Oh, how I love today," says Rose.

"I wish it would never end," says Billy.

Billy and Rose lie back in the grass and think. They think and think, and suddenly, a plan.

"Let's have a sleepover," says Rose.

"In matching pj's," says Billy.

They hop on a swing and get to work on their plan.

"Here's an idea," says Rose. "The sleepover will be at *my* house!" She smiles at Billy.

Billy smiles back. "I have a better idea. The sleepover will be at *my* house!"

"Think yummy, yummy cupcakes. And skating and dancing," adds Rose. "At my house."

"Apples! Bananas! All you can eat," says Billy. "We'll tell scary stories and hide under blankets. At my house."

Rose jumps off the swing. "I hatched the plan," she tells Billy. "*My* house."

Billy waves his arms in the air. "My plan. *My* house."

Rose struts home and slams the door, *bang!*

Billy marches home and slams the door,
bang!

Outside, the night is starry and blinking
and beautiful.

Here in her house, however, Rose is rather pouty. *I want a sleepover.* She peeks out the window. Perhaps Billy will stop by.

But Billy is in his own house, rather pouty himself. *Where, oh, where is Rose?*

A long time passes. It is quiet in the world. And in the quiet of the world, Billy and Rose step into the night, shining flashlights. "Billy, Billy, Billy," in whispers. "Rose, Rose, Rose!"

They cross the yards with blankets and cupcakes, bananas and apples.

"Billy, Billy, Billy!"

"Rose, Rose, Rose!"

And meet in the middle. Their pj's are matching.

"The sleepover could be here in the middle," says Rose.

"Yes," agrees Billy. "Here in the middle."

And that's just where they sleep all through the night.

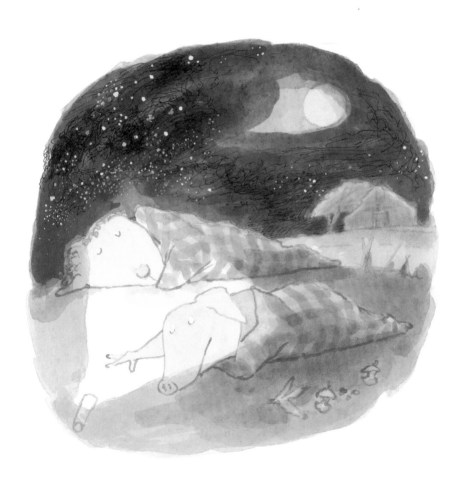